STEP
THIS
WAY
FOR
ANOTHER
GASKITTS
STORY

WELCOME

First published 2002 by Walker Books Ltd
87 Vauxhall Walk, London SE11 5HJ

This edition published 2005

2 4 6 8 10 9 7 5 3 1

This book had been typeset in Stempel Schneider, Cafeteria and Tapioca

Printed and bound in Great Britain by Creative Print and Design (Wales), Ebbw Vale

British Library Cataloguing in Publication Data:
a catalogue record for this book is available from the British Library

ISBN 1-84428-130-2

www.walkerbooks.co.uk

Allan Ahlberg

The Woman Who Won Things

illustrated by
Katharine McEwen

WALKER BOOKS
AND SUBSIDIARIES
LONDON · BOSTON · SYDNEY · AUCKLAND

Contents

Meet The Gaskitts
(and Horace's friend)

Mrs Gaskitt
A taxi-driver
and loving mother
who likes to enter
competitions.

Mr Gaskitt
A fond hard-working
father who always
takes any job
he can get.

Gus and Gloria Gaskitt
Nine-and-a-half-year-old twins.

No, I don't!
Yes, you do!
No, I don't!
Yes, you do!
No, I...
Yes, you...
No...
Yes...

Horace Gaskitt

A ginger-and-white cat
who likes to argue
with his friend.

Horace's Friend

A black cat
who likes to argue
with Horace.

The Gaskitts' Doormat

Sometimes grumpy...

Mostly welcoming...

Sometimes rude...

LOVELY TO SEE YOU!

WIPE YOUR FEET!

BEAT IT!

Chapter One
Mrs Gaskitt's Luck Begins

One morning in the month of May
Mrs Gaskitt got up.

Good morning, Mrs Gaskitt!

She came downstairs, gave Horace a bowl
of Crunchy Mice
and gave his
friend one too.
He was there
on a visit.

Thanks, Mrs
Gaskitt!

Mrs Gaskitt got
Gus and Gloria up,
gave *them* their breakfasts
and sent them off to school.
She read the paper,
drank a cup of tea,
picked up the post
as it came tumbling
through the letterbox,
opened the door...

...and kissed the postman!

But what about *Mr* Gaskitt?

Never mind –

he *was* the postman.

It was his latest job.

Meanwhile, Gus and Gloria were in the
playground watching – Oh no! – their poor
teacher, Mrs Fritter, falling off her bike
at the school gates.

Mrs Fritter hit the pavement
with a terrible bang,
got some nasty cuts and bruises
on her arms and legs, and had to go home.

Back in the kitchen,
Mrs Gaskitt was opening the post.
There was a gas bill
and a phone bill
and a postcard from
Grandma Gaskitt on holiday in Spain.

There was a vet's appointment for Horace ...
and one more envelope.

Mrs Gaskitt opened it.

Congratulations!

Congratulations, Mrs Gaskitt!
said the letter,
*You have won first prize in our
most amazing competition.*

"Wow!" cried Mrs Gaskitt.
"This must be my lucky day."

Chapter Two
One Little Question

Half an hour later, a van
stopped outside the Gaskitts' house.
It had Mrs Gaskitt's prize in it:
A YEAR'S SUPPLY
OF CRUNCHY MICE.

"All I did was answer
one little question," said Mrs Gaskitt.
"Fancy that," said the van man.
"And make up one little caption."

"This must be your lucky day," the van man said.

Mrs Gaskitt's prize filled the kitchen.

Horace's friend was amazed.

So was the doormat.

So was Horace.

"This must be

my lucky day,"

he thought.

WOW!

Back at the school, a supply teacher
had arrived in Gus and Gloria's classroom.

This supply teacher was
rather short
and rather wide.
She had silvery hair,
dangly earrings,
a big smile...

"Hello, dearies!"

...and a huge suitcase.
On wheels.
"My name," she said, "is Mrs Plum."
And she *opened the case*.

16

Meanwhile, back in the kitchen,
Horace and his friend were purring loudly and
gazing up at the piles and piles
of Crunchy Mice.
The word had spread.
Horace's other friends were
at the window, peeping in.

"I bet that lot would
last me ... a year!"
cried Horace.

"Well, it would," said his friend.
"It's a year's supply."

"Oh, yeah," said Horace.

"Or half a year's supply
for two cats," said his friend.

"Yeah," said Horace.

"Or a month's supply
for twelve cats."

"Yeah!"

"Or a day's supply
for three hundred and sixty-five cats!"

"YEAH!"

"Or a *party*," miaowed Horace's friends
from outside. "For us."

Chapter Three
Mrs Plum's Suitcase

Mrs Plum took out of her suitcase:

a ball of wool and some knitting

a photograph in a silver frame

a vase of flowers (plastic)

a small guitar

a sandwich maker

a pair of pink fluffy slippers

and a box of
chocolates.

There was silence in the room.
The children gazed in wonder
at Mrs Plum,
the knitting,
the sandwich maker
and the chocolates.
"This must be *our* lucky day,"
they thought.

Mrs Plum put the flowers
and the photograph on her desk,
and the slippers on her feet.
She opened the box of chocolates
and popped one into her mouth.
"Now then, dearies, let's get started."

The day went by in Mrs Plum's class
and the children loved it.
They had cooking lessons with
the sandwich maker,
science lessons *fixing*
the sandwich maker and
singing lessons with
the guitar.

Mrs Plum read stories to them,
gave them some easy sums
and shared her chocolates.
When the box was empty,
she opened her suitcase
and took out another.

By the end of the day

the children could not believe their luck.

Mrs Plum was the best teacher they had ever had.

The best in the school,

in the town,

in the universe!

Yes, everything was perfect.

Well, *almost* everything.

The only trouble was

that in all the excitement

a few little things ...

had gone missing.

Billy Turpin had lost his football boots.

Tracey Appledrop had lost her pencil case.

Gloria Gaskitt had lost her lucky charm bracelet.

But even then Mrs Plum
was *so* kind
    so helpful
    so sympathetic.
She looked everywhere
in that classroom,
searched high and low,
but with no luck at all.
When home-time came,

the missing things were still missing.

Chapter Four
Mrs Gaskitt's Luck Continues

Two days later, Mrs Gaskitt got up again.

Of course, she got up on the day in between as well, but nothing happened then.

Yes ...

Mrs Gaskitt got up,

Good morning, Mrs Gaskitt!

fed the children,

fed the cats,

Thanks, Mrs Gaskitt!

read the paper,
drank the tea,
heard a familiar sound
out in the street
– Clink, clink! –
opened the door,
picked up the milk...

...and kissed the milkman!
But what about *Mr* Gaskitt?
Never mind –
he *was* the milkman.
It was his very latest job.

Meanwhile – Oh no! – poor Mrs Fritter

was falling over in the doctor's waiting room.

The doctor had just said

she was well enough to return to work.

Now Mrs Fritter had more cuts and bruises

and needed to go back to bed again.

Meanwhile, Mrs Plum was fit and well.

She played football with the boys,

and netball with the girls.

Shoot, dearie!

At playtime, Mrs Plum
drank tea in the staffroom
with the other teachers.

The other teachers liked Mrs Plum.
She told them funny stories
about her long life as a teacher,
shared her chocolates,
and helped them to look for things...

...when they
went missing.

27

Back at the Gaskitts' house,

the phone was ringing.

Mrs Gaskitt was outside washing her taxi.

In she ran and picked up the receiver.

Congratulations!

"Congratulations, Mrs Gaskitt!"

said a man on the phone.

"You have won first prize in our—"

"Wow!" cried Mrs Gaskitt.

"*Another* lucky day."

Chapter Five
One Little Coupon

Two hours later, a lorry
"BEEP, BEEP, I AM REVERSING!"
stopped outside the Gaskitts' house.
It had Mrs Gaskitt's prize in it:
A COMPLETE HOUSEFUL
OF FURNITURE!

"All I did was fill in one
little coupon," said Mrs Gaskitt.

"Well, I never," said the driver.
"And put some ticks in boxes."
"BEEP, BEEP, I AM AMAZED!"

Mrs Gaskitt's prize filled every room in the house
(and the kitchen twice over).
Horace and his friend went round sitting on things.
They were amazed too.

"She's very lucky, my Mrs," said Horace.

"I wonder why."

"Perhaps she's got a lucky horseshoe,"
said his friend. "Or a rabbit's foot –
or a four-leaf clover."

"Or a ten-leaf clover," said Horace.

"There's no such thing," said
his friend.

"Yes, there is."

"No, there isn't."

"Yes, there is."

Yes, there is.

Meanwhile, back at the school,

it was almost home-time.

Some of the children had their coats on,

some were lined up by the door

and some...

...were looking for things.

Gus and Gloria were giving
Randolph, the class rat,
some clean water
and a slice of carrot.

"Now then, dearies," said Mrs Plum.

"Before you go – a message.

I'm planning a little trip soon—"

"Hooray!"

"Great, Miss!"

"I love a trip!"

"Where to, Miss?"

"Where we going?"

"Er ... somewhere nice," said Mrs Plum.

"A sort of mystery tour."

"Brilliant!"

"A mystery tour!"

"I love a mystery tour!"

"I've been on one before!"

"I've been on two!"

"Bring £10," Mrs Plum said.

"Tomorrow, if you can."

"I can bring £10, Miss!"

"I can bring twenty!"

"A hundred!"

As the children hurried off,
Mrs Plum called after them.

"One last thing – make it *cash*, dearies."

She popped a chocolate
into Billy Turpin's mouth.

"No cheques."

Chapter Six
Two Thousand Pounds!

The next day Mrs Gaskitt won:

a holiday for four

a caravan

a free hairdo

and a packet of Protts!!

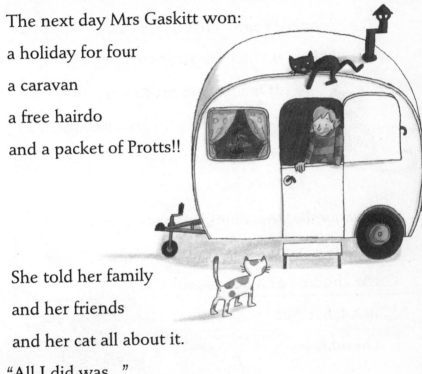

She told her family

and her friends

and her cat all about it.

"All I did was..."

Horace was pleased, of course,
and proud of Mrs Gaskitt.
But he was puzzled too.
"A holiday for *four* – what use is that?
Should be a holiday for five."

"Or six," said his friend.
"Or eleven," said his other friends
outside the window.

Meanwhile, Mrs Plum had collected
twenty-seven £10 notes from
the children and put them
in a safe place.
On wheels.

The children were excited about the trip,

and excited also about the school fete,

only a day away.

Mr Blagg, the headmaster,

made a little speech about it

to the whole school.

There would be book stalls and cake stalls,

raffles and hoop-las,

a coconut-shy and a fancy dress competition.

There'd be a pet show (with prizes),

maypole dancing,

five-a-side for the dads

and an egg-and-spoon race for the mums.

"Last year, children – Sh!" said Mr Blagg,

"– we raised £1,943.78p for the school fund."

"Hooray!" the children yelled.

"Sh!" said Mr Blagg.

"So this time, let's break the record.

Let's make it – Sh!

– two thousand pounds!"

"Hooray!"

"Hooray!"

the children

yelled again.

Just then, up jumped Mrs Plum.

She couldn't stop herself.

"Two thousand pounds!" she cried,

and her big smile filled the hall.

"I'll help!"

Chapter Seven
Some Funny Business

At lunchtime, Mrs Gaskitt
ate her free packet of Protts
and had her free hairdo.
Lucky Mrs Gaskitt.

Meanwhile – Oh no!
– *un*lucky Mrs Fritter.
Mrs Fritter had just popped
into the chemist's for some
painkillers and a bandage.
On her way home and outside the *Travel Agent's*,
she was knocked flying by a short, wide lady
with charming manners,

"Beg pardon, dearie!"

and a huge suitcase.
On wheels.

The lady, however,

was very apologetic and *very* kind.

She helped Mrs Fritter to her feet

and gave her a chocolate.

Later that afternoon,

Gus and Billy Turpin were in the classroom

giving Randolph some exercise.

Gloria and Tracey Appledrop were painting a sign

for the Guess The Weight of the Cake

competition.

Just then a phone rang.

"A phone, Miss! A phone!"

"Who's ringing us?"

"Where is it?"

Well, would you believe it, the phone was ringing
from *inside* Mrs Plum's suitcase.

"It's playing a tune, Miss!"

"So it is, dearie," said Mrs Plum,

and she gave the suitcase a kick.

"I know that tune, Miss!"

"Me too!"

"It's the same as Mr Blagg's phone!"

"Yeah!"

"Only he's *lost* his!"

"So he has, dearie," said Mrs Plum

and she gave the case another kick.

"I helped him look for it."

Meanwhile, Gus and Gloria and some of the

other children were exchanging glances.

There was some funny business here.

Why did Mrs Plum not open the case?

Come to think of it, why did she *never* open it

(apart from that first morning)?

All of a sudden,

the whole class became suspicious.

They smelled a rat, all right ...

and it was *not* Randolph.

Chapter Eight
Handsome Horace

The next day,

which was a Saturday,

Mrs Gaskitt leapt out of bed,

raced downstairs,

flew into the

crowded kitchen:

2 tables

8 chairs

25 cartons of Crunchy Mice,

Good morning, Mrs...

fed the children,
fed Horace,

Thanks, Mrs...

read the paper,
read the post,
opened the back door,
kissed the milkman...

Thanks, Mrs...

...and went red in the face.
It was the *wrong* milkman.

Meanwhile, Gus and Gloria

were grooming Horace.

They brushed his coat till it shone,

tied a new pink ribbon around his neck

and told him how handsome he was.

Horace purred with pride.

He wished his friend

was there to see him.

Later that morning,
Mrs Gaskitt was
still rushing around –
finding her trainers,
boiling an egg –
while Gus and Gloria
followed her about and
tried to get her attention.

"It's that supply teacher, Mum."

"Hm." Mrs Gaskitt was cooling her egg.

"The one with the suitcase."

"Yes." Mrs Gaskitt was
putting her trainers on.

**"Which she
never opens!"**

"Ah." Mrs Gaskitt was
getting a spoon from
the cutlery drawer.
"Well, *we* think..."
Mrs Gaskitt was out
through the door,
"...she's definitely..."
into the garden
and off down the path
with her egg and spoon.

"...up to something!"

Chapter Nine
Mrs Plum Lends a Hand

It was a warm May afternoon.

The school fete was in full swing.

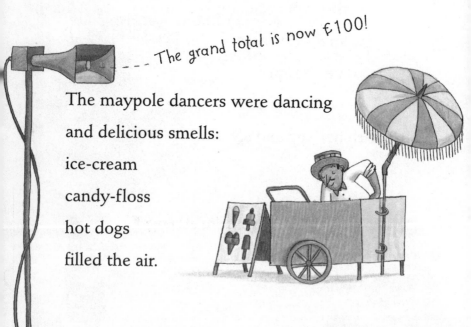

The grand total is now £100!

The maypole dancers were dancing
and delicious smells:

ice-cream

candy-floss

hot dogs

filled the air.

The grand total is now £200!

Mums and dads were working hard.
The infants were rushing
around in their
fancy dress
costumes.

Grand total £250!

Horace, with his beautiful ribbon,
was lined up with the other pets
in the pet show.
And the money...

£300!

...was
pouring
in.

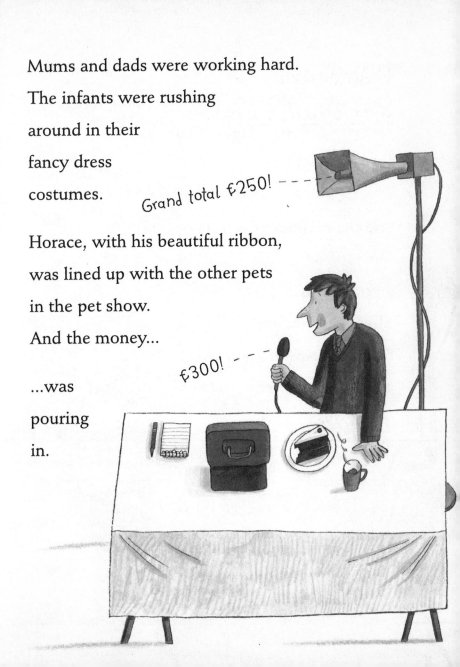

Meanwhile, Mrs Gaskitt was winning things.

She guessed the weight of the cake,

"All I did was..."

and the number of sweets in a jar.

She won a teddy,

a bottle of wine,

three goldfish,

five kilograms of grass seed

and a lawnmower.

1st PRIZE

And Horace saw ... £500! – – – –

most of it.

He purred with pride.

"I know her," he told a guinea pig.

"Oh yes." The guinea pig was not

interested in Mrs Gaskitt.

He had other worries.

"Do I look stupid in this bow?"

"No," said Horace. "Not really."

The guinea pig scowled. "Hm. Bet I do."

MAURICE.   HORACE.   RON.

But, of course, what (you will be wanting to know),
what about Mrs Plum?
Well, Mrs Plum was here,
there and everywhere.
She helped with
the refreshments.

Where's my...?

She helped with
the fancy dress.

Where's...?

She helped with
the coconut-shy.

...?

The children – Gus and Gloria,
Tracey, Billy and the others – followed
Mrs Plum and watched her like hawks.
But the crowds were so big, the noise so loud,
the delicious smells so ... delicious,
that the children didn't *always* see
what she was up to.

Meanwhile, Mr Blagg ...

£1,200!

was looking happier,

£1,300!

and happier,

£1,500!

and happier.

£1,750!

Horace's new friend was looking happier too.

He had just won a rosette.

"So what's your name then?" he asked.

"Horace," said Horace.

"Fancy that – mine's Maurice. Horace and Maurice!"

"Yeah," said Horace, "all we need is a Boris."

"Or a Doris," said Maurice.

"Or a ... Poris," said Horace.

"*Poris?* There's no such name."

"Yes, there is," said Horace.

"No, there isn't."

Yes, there is.

Now, Mrs Gaskitt

and the other mothers were lining up...

£1,900!

£1,999.99!

...for the egg-and-spoon race.

Mr Blagg
jumped on his chair.
"We've made it –
Sh!" he yelled.
"Grand total –
two thousand
pounds!"

"Hooray!" "Hooray!"

The crowd cheered, then cheered again
as the egg-and-spoon race began.

It was a tremendous contest.

First Mrs Turpin was in the lead,

then she dropped her egg.

Then Mrs Appledrop was in the lead

and she dropped her egg.

Then Mrs Gaskitt

was in the lead and...

Meanwhile, all eyes (except two)
were on the race.

The children were watching (and yelling).

Horace was watching (and purring with pride).

Even Mr Blagg on his chair
was watching.

All of a sudden, Mr Blagg looked down
at the table and was *not* happy any more.
The cash box,
the two thousand pounds,
even Mr Blagg's favourite pencil
(which his dear old mother
had given him) ...
had disappeared.

Oh no –
Grand total –
£nil!

Chapter Ten
Oops!

Now, of course, there was uproar

at the school fete.

Everyone was yelling and rushing around.

Well, nearly everyone.

Meanwhile, the egg-and-spoon race

was still in progress.

Mrs Gaskitt got up speed,

while her egg, luckily,

stayed on its spoon.

She ran like the wind,

broke the tape,

won the race, and –

Oh no! – *collided* with a short, wide lady,

silvery hair,

big smile,

suitcase (on wheels)

and knocked her flying.

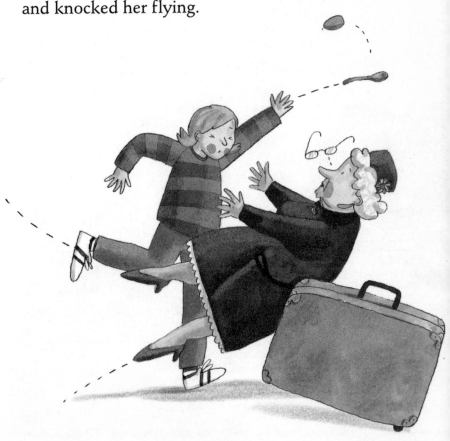

Knocked her
suitcase flying too,
which rolled
and bounced
and rolled again ...
and burst open.

The crowd was astonished...

My umbrella!

Our £2,000!

My football boots!

And all that Mrs Plum, as she sat on the grass with an egg in her lap, could think to say was...

Oops!

Later, when the police arrived, Mrs Plum had rather more to say.

"Can't think what came over me, dearies."

She smiled at Mr Blagg.

"Never done anything like this before."

"Yes, you have," said the inspector.

"Loads of times."

"She's a very clever woman," the inspector explained.

"Thank you, dearie!"

"Robbed more schools than I've had hot dinners. Been on her trail for ages."

The inspector shook hands with Mr Blagg and
congratulated Mrs Gaskitt on her lucky collision.
"This should put a stop to Mrs Plum
(alias Mrs Peach, alias Mrs Pomegranate)
and her little games for a while,
I shouldn't wonder."
He climbed into
his police car.

Chapter Eleven
Mrs Gaskitt's Luck Runs Out

It was a warm May evening.

Mrs Gaskitt walked home

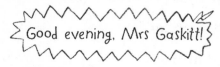

Good evening, Mrs Gaskitt!

with her children,

her cat and her prizes.

Gus and Gloria were telling

their mum all about Mrs Plum.

Mum, Plum – that rhymes!

72

Mrs Gaskitt was telling
Gus and Gloria
(and Horace)
how she had won
the teddy,
the bottle of wine
and all the other things.
"All I did..."

Suddenly, not looking
where she was going,
Mrs Gaskitt walked straight under
a window cleaner's ladder.
Oh no! – *un*lucky Mrs Gaskitt.

Water from the window
cleaner's bucket
came splashing down
and soaked her to the skin.

And that wasn't the end of it.
Next thing, would you believe it,
the *window cleaner himself*
came scrambling down,
grabbed Mrs Gaskitt,
hauled her to her feet –
and kissed her!

But what about *Mr* Gaskitt?
Well, you've guessed it,
haven't you?
Yes – it was
his latest job.

Meanwhile, Horace was thinking hard ...
about luck.

"Hm. Lucky rabbit's foot – no.

Lucky horseshoes – no.

Lucky four-leaf clovers – no.

Lucky black cats..."

It was a warm May night.

The Gaskitts were asleep

in their crowded bedrooms.

The goldfish were getting

used to their new home.

The garage was full of grass seed.

Horace and his friend were

downstairs playing cards.

Snap!

"It's you!" said Horace.

"What is?" said his friend. "SNAP! – I win."

"That's it – you always win!" said Horace.

"You're the *lucky black cat*!"

"No, I'm not – SNAP!" said his friend.

"Yes, you are."

"No, I'm not."

"Yes, you are."

"No, I'm not."

"Yes, you are."

"No, I'm ... not!"

"Yes ... you ... *yawn* ... are."

THAT'S ALL FOLKS!

THE END